Two young men... selves upon Racha A... child. Racha was struck to the heart. At the same moment Hedris was flung backwards, the knife of the second assassin raking at her body. Aidris cried out, everyone was crying out; there was blood, bright blood on the sand of the pathway and a thick gasping sound in her ears.

The noise and violence did not stop. There was a continual shouting, the cries of women, the tramp of feet. She was led through broad, sunlit corridors to the dark bedroom. Hedris lay covered to the neck, her face whiter than the bed linen. Hedris smiled thinly at her daughter; her eyes were wide, as if she strained to see through a mist.

"Quickly," said her mother. "There is a treasure. A secret. Feel the bed frame . . . the carved snake, then the three figures of the Goddess, then the flower . . ."

A small hollow opened two finger breadths from the carved flower in a circle of leaves. Aidris drew out a long, fine chain of bronze; the jewel or medallion on the chain was hidden in a pouch of soft green leather.

CHERRY WILDER
A PRINCESS OF THE CHAMELN

fantasy

A PRINCESS OF THE CHAMELN

Copyright © 1984 by Cherry Wilder.

Published by arrangement with Atheneum Publishers.

A Baen Book

Baen Enterprises
8-10 W. 36th Street
New York, N.Y. 10018

First Baen printing, June 1985

ISBN: 0-671-55966-4

Cover art by Stephen Hickman
Interior map by John M. Ford

Printed in the United States of America

Distributed by
SIMON & SCHUSTER
MASS MERCHANDISE SALES COMPANY
1230 Avenue of the Americas
New York, N.Y. 10020

THE RULERS OF HYLOR

CREST OF THE VAUGUENS OF LIEN

CREST OF THE DUARINGS OF MEL'NIR

Guenna
Markgrafin of Lien- **Edgar Pendark** Prince of Eildon

Ghanor of Mel'Nir

Kelen
Markgraf of Lien
-Zaramund of Grays

CREST OF THE DAINDRU
Rulers of the Chameln lands

Elvedegran of Lien — **Gol**

A Son?

Queen Charis
Am Firn

Micha
Am Firn

Esher
Am Zor-Aravel of Lien

Racha Am Firn-Hedris
of Lien

Sharn Am Zor   **Merilla**   **Carel**

CREST OF THE MENVIRS OF ATHRON

Aidris Am Firn

Duke of Varda-Imelda Golden Hair
   (Imal Am Firn Younger sister of Queen Charis)

Vor Prince of Athron

Prince Flor   **Prince Terril**

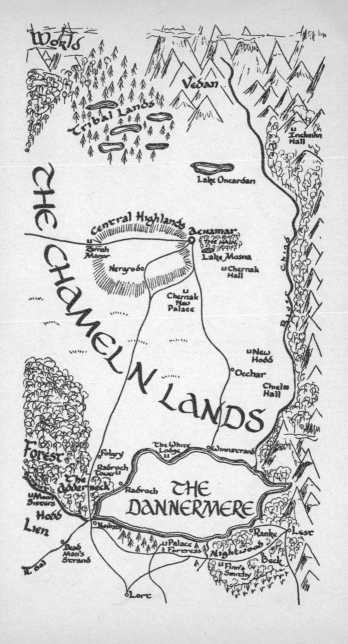